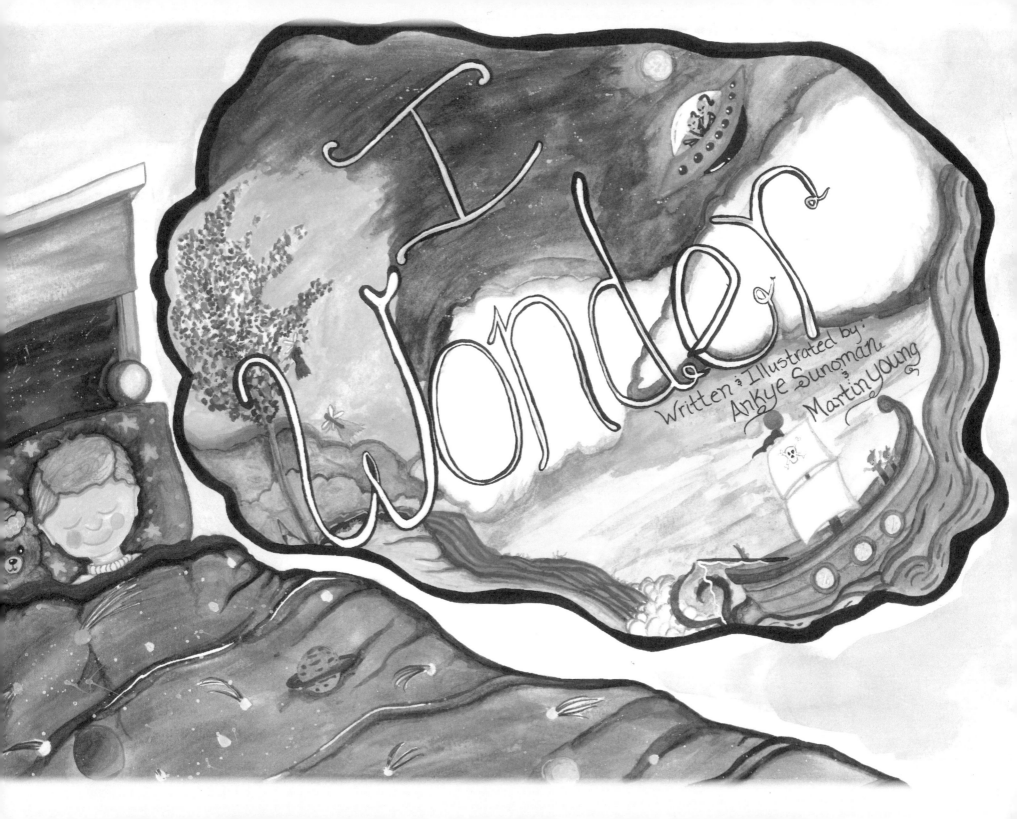

Xulon Press
555 Winderley Pl, Suite 225
Maitland, FL 32751
407.339.4217
www.xulonpress.com

Arranged by Martin Young

Unless otherwise indicated, Scripture quotations taken from (Version(s) used)

Paperback ISBN-13: 978-1-66288-902-8
eBook ISBN-13: 978-1-66288-903-5

Dedication:

To my mother Katherine "Kitty" Young. Thank you for all the love you held for us boys growing up and letting our minds wonder. We miss you and think of you often!

To our children:

We love all 7 of you very much! Please never stop wondering! The possibilities are endless if you just believe!!! Thank you for choosing us to be your parents! Alexanndraea, Abbie, Callaghan, Emrys, Ember, Luka, and Bobby.

I do not count sheep as I fall asleep at night. I would rather wonder about all the THINGS that could be possible.

45 46 47 54 55

A summer fishing adventure the two must map out,
A quest that will surely be fun, without a doubt!
Off into the ocean blue the two do sail,
To catch a mighty-big, friendly beast, they must not fail!
The lad's pole suddenly bent under the weight,
They looked over the bow to see what was their fate.
Behold! A giant, friendly beast was attached to the lad's line.
He was holding many treasures, and, oh, how they did shine!
But the best part was the lovely melody, so pleasing to the ear,
The beast was playing a trumpet so brilliant and so clear!

I WONDER
Do grandpa pirates teach their grandpirates how to fish?!?
ARGH!!! You have hooked a big one Cal!
ARGH! I Shore have gramps!
The Stew Crew

Grandma Dragon is sitting cozily in her cave,
Knitting away her long, cold wintery days.
She's working carefully on some socks in her loving ways,
Staying close to the fire without setting them ablaze!
Her nose has a bit of a tickle, and she's trying hard not to sneeze.
If she does, her grandson Stevie will have nothing to cover his knees!
She is drinking hot cocoa from her handmade mug made with love,
Thinking about the special dragon in the picture on the wall
holding his favorite glove.
Every stitch she counts and knits with such grace and tender care,
Her needles clinking away with each stitch until she
has a perfect knitted pair.
Her grandson dragon is on his way over to her mountain cave.
She can't wait to see him come bounding in with his big toothy grin
and his gleeful wave.

Bigfoots love to brush and keep their big teeth pearly white.
It's the last thing they do before they're tucked in for the night.
Then the first thing they do after breakfast each day,
Is brush their Bigfoot teeth before they even play!
Sometimes they brush their teeth just for fun.
They even brush their teeth after a great big run!
Healthy teeth is what all Bigfoots live for.
That is what we call common knowledge folklore.

I WONDER
Do lil bigfoots have to brush their teeth?!?
DREAM BIG
HEIDI
Love You
I AM ALWAYS WITH YOU Little Hoot!
EMBER
G
H
SOAP

The school bells are ringing, singing through the crisp morning air.

Letting the troll children know to be seated in their chairs.

Time to read about the world and learn all there is to know.

To answer questions the children have, like "Why do we have a shadow?"

"Do our shadows follow us under the bridge, everywhere we go?"

"Do our shadows go fast when we run across the bridge,

or do they take it slow?"

They want their many questions answered by the end of day.

When the bell rings, they can run off,

their shadows trailing behind to play.

It is time to turn on the anti-gravity control system and
clean up our family space car.
It takes us all to different places in the galaxy near and far.
We travel at light speed to school, soccer games, dance lessons,
and sometimes the store.
"Teamwork makes the dream work" is a song we sing while
we do our daily chores.
Many things are left behind in our hurry and scurry of everyday living.
Helping your family do the daily chores in life is very giving.

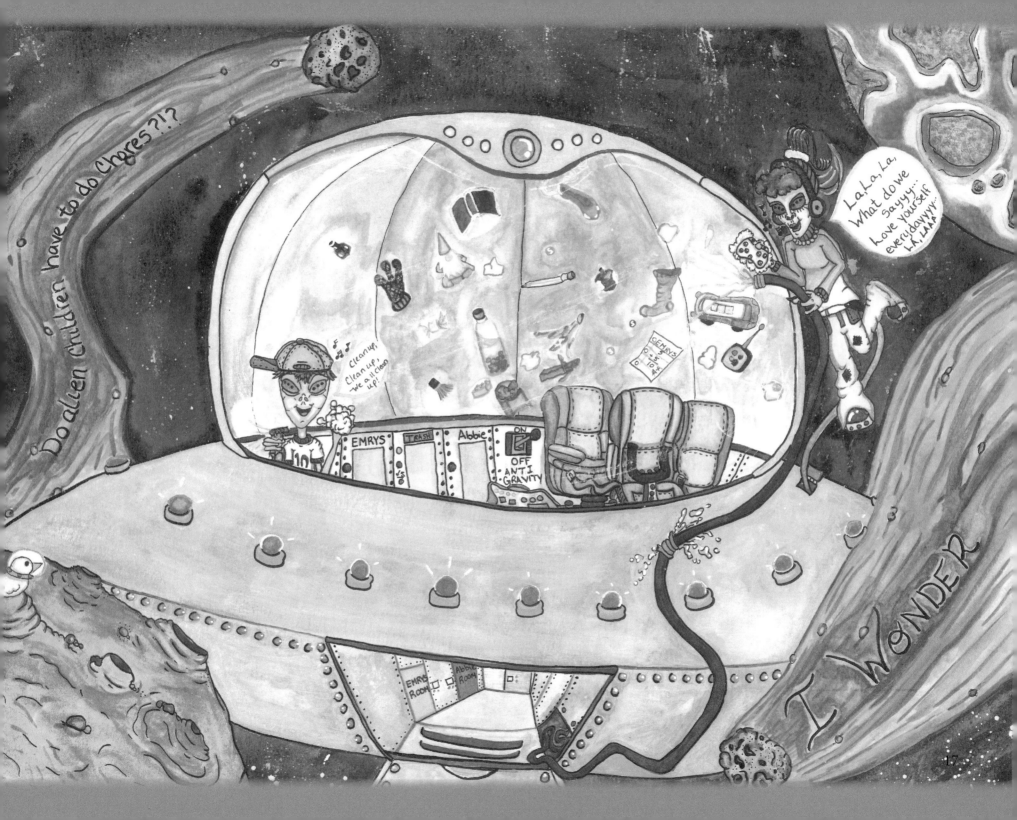

Snowflakes are falling and tumbling from the sky.

The Snowman's family is filled with joy—they wonder who might stop by!

The children sing songs as they set up their Frozen roadside store.

Frozen lemonade, popsicles, snow cones, and more!

The family's dog, Puddles, is excitedly wagging his tail.

It's time for the Frozen Lemonade stand to open and have its sale!

Come on over for a frozen treat filled with love,

As the snow continues to fall gracefully from the beautiful sky above.

I Wonder
Do Snowmen Sell frozen Lemonade?
I SNOW It will be a wonderful DAY!
FROZEN LEMONADE
Tell us about one thing you learned in school today for a special TREAT!
I can not wait to hear what the Children learned at school today. I hope they have found a groundbreaking hypothesICE!
To: ALLIE

Broccoli, carrots, turnips, squash, beets, green beans, and corn.
Oh, my beautiful fairy children, why do your faces look so forlorn?
If you give this bountiful harvest a chance and just try it,
then you will see!
All I have put in front of you tastes so delicious that
your faces will be filled with glee.
Different textures, tastes, and colors your palates are lucky to try.
The flavors that will dance on your tongues surely will not lie.
You will fall in love with the vegetables and all they have to give.
Now eat them up, young fairy ones, they help us all to live.

Scrub a dub dub, there are ducks, boats, and Maximus Gnome in the tub.
It is time to give his face, toes, and ears a really good scrub.
He lathers the soap on his rag until the bubbles float all around.
Father Gnome sits, after a long day's work, in the background.
He is listening to his favorite tunes while he thinks about his day.
When he turns with words of wisdom and Maximus hears him say,
"Do not forget to wash behind your ears, Maximus, or things will grow."
Maximus wonders what those things could be, and
now he really wants to know.
Using his imagination, he ponders on what might grow
if he was not to listen.
He then decides not to take that chance and
scrubs until his ears glisten!

I WONDER
Do gnome fathers make their children wash behind their ears?!?
Maximus, Please do not forget to wash behind your ears!
Yes! Sir! I will not forget to get behind my ears father.
I wonder if human children have to wash behind their ears?
SOAP

Hip hip hooray!
It is your special day!
Family and friends have traveled from afar.
Some came by hot air balloons, some by train, and others by car.
They came to celebrate you, and they would like to say,
Hip hip hooray! Have a happy birthday!

25

As we lie down to sleep tonight,
We pray for the world with all our might.
We pray for it to have peace, happiness, and grace.
We pray everyone all over the world has a safe sleeping space.
We pray for you, we pray for them, we pray for all.
We pray for the really big, and we pray for the very small.
We love each of you in every way.
We pray for you at the end of every single day!

Does Jesus tuck the angels in at night?

And whisper words that let them know everything's all right?

The day is done, and night is here.

It is time to tuck in the ones so dear.

The beautiful angels who keep watch over my flock.

My angels that follow you on your walk.

It is time for them to sleep while you rest.

So tomorrow, you both will be at your best.

I love each of you in every way.

Goodnight, my children, I will see you on the new day.

I Wonder

Does Jesus tuck
in the angels?

Milton Keynes UK
Ingram Content Group UK Ltd.
UKRC031005280224
438626UK00002B/2

* 9 7 8 1 6 6 2 8 8 9 0 2 8 *

Max does not like to count sheep as he falls asleep. Max likes to wonder about all the different possibilities that could be happening in the world. He wonders about pirate grandpas, angels praying and unicorn birthdays. Join Max before bed and wonder with him until you drift off to sleep. Can you spot the ducks?

Martin and Ankye are a duo with a mission. A mission to bring new great, wholesome books to the children of the world. Books that help kids keep their imagination alive with morals built into the stories. "I Wonder" is their first book they have written together as a team. Martin was born and raised in Upstate New York. Ankye was born and raised in Kansas. The two crossed paths and the rest is history. News about their books and upcoming books can be found at https://ankyesunoman.com

ISBN 978-1-6628-8902-8

90000

xulon
PRESS

9 781662 889028

Perfectly Petra

Amber Hayden Dixon